LITTLE HOUSE SISTERS

Collected Stories from the Little House Books

BY

LAURA INGALLS WILDER

ILLUSTRATED BY

GARTH WILLIAMS

HarperCollins*Publishers*

Little House Sisters
Collected Stories from the Little House Books
Copyright © 1997 by HarperCollins Publishers, Inc.

Text adapted from the following books:
Little House in the Big Woods, text copyright 1932, copyright renewed 1959, Roger Lea MacBride; pictures copyright 1953 by Garth Williams, renewed 1981 by Garth Williams. *Little House on the Prairie*, text copyright 1935, copyright renewed 1963, Roger Lea MacBride; pictures copyright 1953 by Garth Williams, renewed 1981 by Garth Williams. *On the Banks of Plum Creek*, text copyright 1937, copyright renewed 1965, Roger Lea MacBride; pictures copyright 1953 by Garth Williams, renewed 1981 by Garth Williams. *By the Shores of Silver Lake*, text copyright 1939, copyright renewed 1967, Roger Lea MacBride; pictures copyright 1953 by Garth Williams, renewed 1981 by Garth Williams. *Little Town on the Prairie*, text copyright 1941, copyright renewed 1969, Roger Lea MacBride; pictures copyright 1953 by Garth Williams, renewed 1981 by Garth Williams. *These Happy Golden Years*, text copyright 1943, copyright renewed 1971, Roger Lea MacBride; pictures copyright 1953 by Garth Williams, renewed 1981 by Garth Williams.

Library of Congress Cataloging-in-Publication Data
Wilder, Laura Ingalls, 1867–1957.
    Little house sisters: collected stories from the Little house books / by Laura Ingalls Wilder ;
illustrated by Garth Williams.
        p.   cm.
    Summary: A collection of stories describing the adventures Laura Ingalls Wilder and her sisters shared while growing up in frontier communities in the Middle West.
    ISBN 0-06-027587-1. — ISBN 0-06-027670-3 (lib. bdg.)
    [1. Frontier and pioneer life—Fiction.   2. Family life—Fiction.   3. Sisters—Fiction.]
I. Williams, Garth, ill.   II. Title.
PZ7.W6461Liu   1997   96-34742
[Fic]—dc20   CIP
                                                                                        AC

1 2 3 4 5 6 7 8 9 10

First Edition

CONTENTS

ONCE UPON A TIME, *a little girl named Laura Ingalls lived in a little log cabin in the Big Woods of Wisconsin with her Pa, her Ma, her big sister, Mary, and her baby sister Carrie. Laura had many adventures as she traveled west across the prairie with her family in their covered wagon, and when Laura was grown, she told the stories of her childhood in the Little House books. Some of the most wonderful stories in these books are those celebrating the special moments Laura experienced growing up with her sisters, Mary, Carrie, and Grace. From their adventures in the Big Woods, on the prairie, by the beautiful banks of Plum Creek, and by the shores of Silver Lake to those later on in the little town of De Smet, South Dakota, here are some of the most special times Laura shared with her sisters.*

In the Big Woods

Laura, Mary, and Baby Carrie are just little girls and are living in the Big Woods of Wisconsin in a little log cabin. There are no roads, houses, or people around them, but Laura and Mary have each other, and together they run and play outdoors among the tall trees and the green grass. Each morning Pa goes out hunting, and Laura and Mary help Ma with the chores. At night, when Pa comes home, Laura and Mary run to him and climb up on his knees. It is a happy time for Laura and Mary, as they discover how lucky they are to have a sister for a best friend!

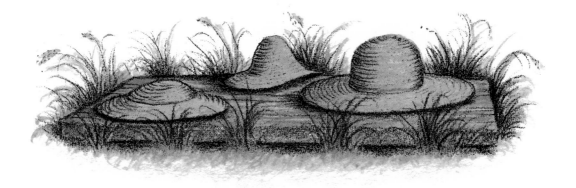

Summertime

Now it was summertime, and people went visiting. Sometimes Uncle Henry, or Uncle George, or Grandpa, came riding out of the Big Woods to see Pa. Ma would come to the door and ask how all the folks were, and she would say:

"Charles is in the clearing."

Then she would cook more dinner than usual, and dinner time would be longer. Pa and Ma and the visitor would sit talking a little while before they went back to work.

Sometimes Ma let Laura and Mary go across the road and down the hill, to see

Mrs. Peterson. The Petersons had just moved in. Their house was new, and always very neat, because Mrs. Peterson had no little girls to muss it up. She was a Swede, and she let Laura and Mary look at the pretty things she had brought from Sweden—laces, and colored embroideries, and china.

Mrs. Peterson talked Swedish to them, and they talked English to her, and they understood each other perfectly. She always gave them each a cookie when they left, and they nibbled the cookies very slowly while they walked home.

Laura nibbled away exactly half of hers, and Mary nibbled exactly half of hers, and the other halves they saved for Baby Carrie. Then when they got home, Carrie had two half-cookies, and that was a whole cookie.

This wasn't right. All they wanted to do was to divide the cookies fairly with Carrie. Still, if Mary saved half her cookie, while Laura ate the whole of hers, or if Laura saved half, and Mary ate her whole cookie, that wouldn't be fair, either.

They didn't know what to do. So each saved half, and gave it to Baby Carrie. But they always felt that somehow that wasn't quite fair.

Sometimes a neighbor sent word that the family was coming to spend the day. Then Ma did extra cleaning and cooking, and opened the package of store sugar. And on the day set, a wagon would come driving up to the gate in the morning and there would be strange children to play with.

When Mr. and Mrs. Huleatt came, they brought Eva and Clarence with them.

Eva was a pretty girl, with dark eyes and black curls. She played carefully and kept her dress clean and smooth. Mary liked that, but Laura liked better to play with Clarence.

Clarence was red-headed and freckled, and always laughing. His clothes were pretty, too. He wore a blue suit buttoned all the way up the front with bright gilt buttons, and trimmed with braid, and he had copper-toed shoes. The strips of copper across the toes were so glittering bright that Laura wished she were a boy. Little girls didn't wear copper-toes. Laura and Clarence ran and shouted and climbed trees, while Mary and Eva walked nicely together and talked. Ma and Mrs. Huleatt visited and looked at a *Godey's Lady's Book* which

Mrs. Huleatt had brought, and Pa and Mr. Huleatt looked at the horses and the crops and smoked their pipes.

Once Aunt Lotty came to spend the day. That morning Laura had to stand still a long time while Ma unwound her hair from the cloth strings and combed it into long curls. Mary was all ready, sitting primly on a chair, with her golden curls shining and her china-blue dress fresh and crisp.

Laura liked her own red dress. But Ma pulled her hair dreadfully, and it was brown instead of golden, so that no one noticed it. Everyone noticed and admired Mary's.

"There!" Ma said at last. "Your hair is curled beautifully, and Lotty is coming. Run meet her, both of you, and ask her which she likes best, brown curls or golden curls."

Laura and Mary ran out of the door and down the path, for Aunt Lotty was already at the gate. Aunt Lotty was a big girl, much taller than Mary. Her dress was a beautiful pink and she was swinging a pink sunbonnet by one string.

"Which do you like best, Aunt Lotty," Mary asked, "brown curls, or golden curls?" Ma had told them to ask that, and Mary was a very good little girl who always did exactly as she was told.

Laura waited to hear what Aunt Lotty would say, and she felt miserable.

"I like both kinds best," Aunt Lotty said, smiling. She took Laura and Mary

by the hand, one on either side, and they danced along to the door where Ma stood.

The sunshine came streaming through the windows into the house, and everything was so neat and pretty. The table was covered with a red cloth, and the cookstove was polished shining black. Through the bedroom door Laura could see the trundle bed in its place under the big bed. The pantry door stood wide open, giving the sight and smell of goodies on the shelves, and Black Susan came purring down the stairs from the attic, where she had been taking a nap.

It was all so pleasant, and Laura felt so gay and good that no one would ever have thought she could be as naughty as she was that evening.

Aunt Lotty had gone, and Laura and Mary were tired and cross. They were at the woodpile, gathering a pan of chips to kindle the fire in the morning. They always hated to pick up chips, but every day they had to do it. Tonight they hated it more than ever.

Laura grabbed the biggest chip, and Mary said:

"I don't care. Aunt Lotty likes my hair best, anyway. Golden hair is lots prettier than brown."

Laura's throat swelled tight, and she could not speak. She knew golden hair was prettier than brown. She couldn't speak, so she reached out quickly and slapped Mary's face.

Then she heard Pa say, "Come here, Laura."

She went slowly, dragging her feet. Pa was sitting just inside the door. He had seen her slap Mary.

"You remember," Pa said, "I told you girls you must never strike each other."

Laura began, "But Mary said—"

"That makes no difference," said Pa. "It is what I say that you must mind."

Then he took down a strap from the wall, and he whipped Laura with the strap.

Laura sat on a chair in the corner and sobbed. When she stopped sobbing, she sulked. The only thing in the whole world to be glad about was that Mary had to fill the chip pan all by herself.

At last, when it was getting dark, Pa said again, "Come here, Laura." His voice was kind, and when Laura came he took her on his knee and hugged her close. She sat in the crook of his arm, her head against his shoulder and his long brown whiskers partly covering her eyes, and everything was all right again.

She told Pa all about it, and she asked him, "You don't like golden hair better than brown, do you?"

Pa's blue eyes shone down at her, and he said, "Well, Laura, my hair is brown."

She had not thought of that. Pa's hair was brown, and his whiskers were brown, and she thought brown was a lovely color. But she was glad that Mary had had to gather all the chips.

Winter Days and Winter Nights

The first snow came, and the bitter cold. Every morning Pa took his gun and his traps and was gone all day in the Big Woods, setting the small traps for muskrats and mink along the creeks, the middle-sized traps for foxes and wolves in the woods. He set out the big bear traps hoping to get a fat bear before they all went into their dens for the winter.

One morning he came back, took the horses and sled, and hurried away again. He had shot a bear. Laura and Mary jumped up and down and clapped their hands, they were so glad. Mary shouted:

"I want the drumstick! I want the drumstick!"

Mary did not know how big a bear's drumstick is.

When Pa came back he had both a bear and a pig in the wagon. He had been going through the woods, with a big bear trap in his hands and the gun on his shoulder, when he walked around a big pine tree covered with snow, and the bear was behind the tree.

The bear had just killed the pig and was picking it up to eat it. Pa said the bear was standing up on its hind legs, holding the pig in its paws just as though they were hands.

Pa shot the bear, and there was no way of knowing where the pig came from nor whose pig it was.

"So I just brought home the bacon," Pa said.

There was plenty of fresh meat to last for a long time. The days and the nights were so cold that the pork in a box and the bear meat hanging in the little shed outside the back door were solidly frozen and did not thaw.

When Ma wanted fresh meat for dinner Pa took the ax and cut off a chunk of frozen bear meat or pork. But the sausage balls, or the salt pork, or the smoked hams and the venison, Ma could get for herself from the shed or the attic.

The snow kept coming till it was drifted and banked against the house. In the mornings the window panes were covered with frost in beautiful pictures of trees and flowers and fairies.

Ma said that Jack Frost came in the night and made the pictures, while everyone was asleep. Laura thought that Jack Frost was a little man all snowy white, wearing a glittering white pointed cap and soft white knee-boots made of deer-skin. His coat was white and his mittens were white, and he did not carry a gun on his back, but in his hands he had shining sharp tools with which he carved the pictures.

Laura and Mary were allowed to take Ma's thimble and make pretty patterns of circles in the frost on the glass. But they never spoiled the pictures that Jack Frost had made in the night.

When they put their mouths close to the pane and blew their breath on it, the

white frost melted and ran in drops down the glass. Then they could see the drifts of snow outdoors and the great trees standing bare and black, making thin blue shadows on the white snow.

Laura and Mary helped Ma with the work. Every morning there were the dishes to wipe. Mary wiped more of them than Laura because she was bigger, but Laura always wiped carefully her own little cup and plate.

By the time the dishes were all wiped and set away, the trundle bed was aired. Then, standing one on each side, Laura and Mary straightened the covers, tucked them in well at the foot and the sides, plumped up the pillows and put them in place. Then Ma pushed the trundle bed into its place under the big bed.

After this was done, Ma began the work that belonged to that day. Each day had its own proper work. Ma used to say:

> *"Wash on Monday,*
>
> *Iron on Tuesday,*
>
> *Mend on Wednesday,*
>
> *Churn on Thursday,*
>
> *Clean on Friday,*
>
> *Bake on Saturday,*
>
> *Rest on Sunday."*

Laura liked the churning and the baking days best of all the week.

In winter the cream was not yellow as it was in summer, and butter churned from it was white and not so pretty. Ma liked everything on her table to be pretty, so in the wintertime she colored the butter.

After she had put the cream in the tall crockery churn and set it near the stove to warm, she washed and scraped a long orange-colored carrot. Then she grated it on the bottom of the old, leaky tin pan that Pa had punched full of nail-holes for her. Ma rubbed the carrot across the roughness until she had

rubbed it all through the holes, and when she lifted up the pan, there was a soft, juicy mound of grated carrot.

She put this in a little pan of milk on the stove and when the milk was hot she poured milk and carrot into a cloth bag. Then she squeezed the bright yellow milk into the churn, where it colored all the cream. Now the butter would be yellow.

Laura and Mary were allowed to eat the carrot after the milk had been squeezed out. Mary thought she ought to have the larger share because she was older, and Laura said she should have it because she was littler. But Ma said they must divide it evenly. It was very good.

When the cream was ready, Ma scalded the long wooden churn-dash, put it in the churn, and dropped the wooden churn-cover over it. The churn-cover had a little round hole in the middle, and Ma moved the dash up and down, up and down, through the hole.

She churned for a long time. Mary could sometimes churn while Ma rested, but the dash was too heavy for Laura.

At first the splashes of cream showed thick and smooth around the little hole. After a long time, they began to look grainy. Then Ma churned more slowly, and on the dash there began to appear tiny grains of yellow butter.

When Ma took off the churn-cover, there was the butter in a golden lump, drowning in the buttermilk. Then Ma took out the lump with a wooden paddle, into a wooden bowl, and she washed it many times in cold water, turning it over and over and working it with the paddle until the water ran clear. After that she salted it.

Now came the best part of the churning. Ma molded the butter. On the loose bottom of the wooden butter-mold was carved the picture of a strawberry with two strawberry leaves.

With the paddle Ma packed butter tightly into the mold until it was full. Then she turned it upside-down over a plate, and pushed on the handle of the loose bottom. The little, firm pat of golden butter came out, with the strawberry and its leaves molded on the top.

Laura and Mary watched, breathless, one on each side of Ma, while the golden little butter-pats, each with its strawberry on the top, dropped onto the plate as Ma put all the butter through the mold. Then Ma gave them each a drink of good, fresh buttermilk.

On Saturdays, when Ma made the bread, they each had a little piece of dough to make into a little loaf. They might have a bit of cookie dough, too, to make little cookies, and once Laura even made a pie in her patty-pan.

After the day's work was done, Ma sometimes cut paper dolls for them. She cut the dolls out of stiff white paper, and drew the faces with a pencil. Then from bits of colored paper she cut dresses and hats, ribbons and laces, so that Laura and Mary could dress their dolls beautifully.

But the best time of all was at night, when Pa came home.

He would come in from his tramping through the snowy woods with tiny icicles hanging on the ends of his mustaches. He would hang his gun on the wall over the door, throw off his fur cap and coat and mittens, and call: "Where's my little half-pint of sweet cider half drunk up?"

That was Laura, because she was so small.

Laura and Mary would run to climb on his knees and sit there while he warmed himself by the fire. Then he would put on his coat and cap and mittens again and go out to do the chores and bring in plenty of wood for the fire.

Sometimes, when Pa had walked his traplines quickly because the traps were empty, or when he had got some game sooner than usual, he would come home early. Then he would have time to play with Laura and Mary.

One game they loved was called mad dog. Pa would run his fingers through his thick, brown hair, standing it all up on end. Then he dropped on all

fours and, growling, he chased Laura and Mary all around the room, trying to get them cornered where they couldn't get away.

They were quick at dodging and running, but once he caught them against the wood-box, behind the stove. They couldn't get past Pa, and there was no other way out.

Then Pa growled so terribly, his hair was so wild and his eyes so fierce that it all seemed real. Mary was so frightened that she could not move. But as Pa came nearer Laura screamed, and with a wild leap and a scramble she went over the wood-box, dragging Mary with her.

And at once there was no mad dog at all. There was only Pa standing there with his blue eyes shining, looking at Laura.

"Well!" he said to her. "You're only a little half-pint of cider half drunk up, but by Jinks! you're as strong as a little French horse!"

"You shouldn't frighten the children so, Charles," Ma said. "Look how big their eyes are."

Pa looked, and then he took down his fiddle. He began to play and sing.

> *"Yankee Doodle went to town,*
>
> *He wore his striped trousies,*
>
> *He swore he couldn't see the town,*
>
> *There was so many houses."*

Laura and Mary forgot all about the mad dog.

> *"And there he saw some great big guns,*
>
> *Big as a log of maple,*
>
> *And every time they turned 'em round,*
>
> *It took two yoke of cattle.*
>
> *"And every time they fired 'em off,*
>
> *It took a horn of powder,*
>
> *It made a noise like father's gun,*
>
> *Only a nation louder."*

Pa was keeping time with his foot, and Laura clapped her hands to the music when he sang,

> *"And I'll sing Yankee Doodle-de-do,*
>
> *And I'll sing Yankee Doodle,*
>
> *And I'll sing Yankee Doodle-de-do,*
>
> *And I'll sing Yankee Doodle!"*

All alone in the wild Big Woods, and the snow, and the cold, the little log house was warm and snug and cosy. Pa and Ma and Mary and Laura and Baby Carrie were comfortable and happy there, especially at night.

Exploring the Open Prairie

As Laura and her sisters grow, so too does the number of people settling in the Big Woods. Pa decides it is time to move on, and Laura, Ma and Pa, Mary and Baby Carrie, and their good old bulldog, Jack, travel west by covered wagon and settle on the Kansas prairie. The Ingalls sisters soon discover there is plenty of fun and adventure to be found on the prairie—the birds' nests in the tall prairie grass, the scurrying gophers, the gray rabbits, and the curious prairie dogs. It's a whole new world for Laura, Mary, and Baby Carrie as they explore their new home on the prairie.

Indian Camp

Day after day was hotter than the day before. The wind was hot. "As if it came out of an oven," Ma said.

The grass was turning yellow. The whole world was rippling green and gold under the blazing sky.

At noon the wind died. No birds sang. Everything was so still that Laura could hear the squirrels chattering in the trees down by the creek. Suddenly black crows flew overhead, cawing their rough, sharp caws. Then everything was still again.

Ma said that this was midsummer.

Pa wondered where the Indians had gone. He said they had left their little camp on the prairie. And one day he asked Laura and Mary if they would like to see that camp.

Laura jumped up and down and clapped her hands, but Ma objected.

"It is so far, Charles," she said. "And in this heat."

Pa's blue eyes twinkled. "This heat doesn't hurt the Indians and it won't hurt us," he said. "Come on, girls!"

"Please, can't Jack come, too?" Laura begged. Pa had taken his gun, but he looked at Laura and he looked at Jack, then he looked at Ma, and he put the gun up on its pegs again.

"All right, Laura," he said. "I'll take Jack, Caroline, and leave you the gun."

Jack jumped around them, wagging his stump of a tail. As soon as he saw which way they were going, he set off, trotting ahead. Pa came next and behind him came Mary, and then Laura. Mary kept her sunbonnet on, but Laura let hers dangle down her back.

The ground was hot under their bare feet. The sunshine pierced through their faded dresses and tingled on their arms and backs. The air was really as hot as the air in an oven, and it smelled faintly like baking bread. Pa said the smell came from all the grass seeds parching in the heat.

They went farther and farther into the vast prairie. Laura felt smaller and

smaller. Even Pa did not seem as big as he really was. At last they went down into the little hollow where the Indians had camped.

Jack started up a big rabbit. When it bounded out of the grass Laura jumped. Pa said, quickly: "Let him go, Jack! We have meat enough." So Jack sat down and watched the big rabbit go bounding away down the hollow.

Laura and Mary looked around them. They stayed close to Pa. Low bushes grew on the sides of the hollow—buck-brush with sprays of berries faintly pink, and sumac holding up green cones but showing here and there a bright red leaf. The goldenrod's plumes were turning gray, and the ox-eyed daisies' yellow petals hung down from the crown centers.

All this was hidden in the secret little hollow. From the house Laura had seen nothing but grasses, and now from this hollow she could not see the house. The prairie seemed to be level, but it was not level.

Laura asked Pa if there were lots of hollows on the prairie, like this one. He said there were.

"Are Indians in them?" she almost whispered. He said he didn't know. There might be.

She held tight to his hand and Mary held to his other hand, and they looked at the Indians' camp. There were ashes where Indian camp fires had been. There were holes in the ground where tent-poles had been driven. Bones were scattered

where Indian dogs had gnawed them. All along the sides of the hollow, Indian ponies had bitten the grasses short.

Tracks of big moccasins and smaller moccasins were everywhere, and tracks of little bare toes. And over these tracks were tracks of rabbits and tracks of birds, and wolves' tracks.

Pa read the tracks for Mary and Laura. He showed them tracks of two middle-sized moccasins by the edge of a camp fire's ashes. An Indian woman had squatted there. She wore a leather skirt with fringes; the tiny marks of the fringe were in the dust. The track of her toes inside the moccasins was deeper than the track of her heels, because she had leaned forward to stir something cooking in a pot on the fire.

Then Pa picked up a smoke-blackened forked stick. And he said that the pot had hung from a stick laid across the top of two upright, forked sticks. He showed Mary and Laura the holes where the forked sticks had been driven into the

ground. Then he told them to look at the bones around that camp fire and tell him what had cooked in that pot.

They looked, and they said, "Rabbit." That was right; the bones were rabbits' bones.

Suddenly Laura shouted, "Look! Look!" Something bright blue glittered in the dust. She picked it up, and it was a beautiful blue bead. Laura shouted with joy.

Then Mary saw a red bead, and Laura saw a green one, and they forgot everything but beads. Pa helped them look. They found white beads and brown beads, and more and more red and blue beads. All that afternoon they hunted for beads in the dust of the Indian camp. Now and then Pa walked up to the edge of the hollow and looked toward home, then he came back and helped to hunt for more beads. They looked all the ground over carefully.

When they couldn't find any more, it was almost sunset. Laura had a handful of beads, and so did Mary. Pa tied them carefully in his handkerchief, Laura's

beads in one corner and Mary's in another corner. He put the handkerchief in his pocket, and they started home.

The sun was low behind their backs when they came out of the hollow. Home was small and very far away. And Pa did not have his gun.

Pa walked so swiftly that Laura could hardly keep up. She trotted as fast as she could, but the sun sank faster. Home seemed farther and farther away. The prairie seemed larger, and a wind ran over it, whispering something frightening. All the grasses shook as if they were scared.

Then Pa turned around and his blue eyes twinkled at Laura. He said: "Getting tired, little half-pint? It's a long way for little legs."

He picked her up, big girl that she was, and he settled her safe against his shoulder. He took Mary by the hand, and so they all came home together.

Supper was cooking on the fire, Ma was setting the table, and Baby Carrie played with little pieces of wood on the floor. Pa tossed the handkerchief to Ma.

"I'm later than I meant, Caroline," he said. "But look what the girls found." He took the milk-bucket and went quickly to bring Pet and Patty from their picket-lines and to milk the cow.

Ma untied the handkerchief and exclaimed at what she found. The beads were even prettier than they had been in the Indian camp.

Laura stirred her beads with her finger and watched them sparkle and shine. "These are mine," she said.

Then Mary said, "Carrie can have mine."

Ma waited to hear what Laura would say. Laura didn't want to say anything. She wanted to keep those pretty beads. Her chest felt all hot inside, and she wished with all her might that Mary wouldn't always be such a good little girl. But she couldn't let Mary be better than she was.

So she said, slowly, "Carrie can have mine, too."

"That's my unselfish, good little girls," said Ma.

She poured Mary's beads into Mary's hands, and Laura's into Laura's hands, and she said she would give them a thread to string them on. The beads would make a pretty necklace for Carrie to wear around her neck.

Mary and Laura sat side by side on their bed, and they strung those pretty beads on the thread that Ma gave them. Each wet her end of the thread in her mouth and twisted it tightly. Then Mary put her end of the thread through the small hole in each of the beads, and Laura put her end through her beads, one by one.

They didn't say anything. Perhaps Mary felt sweet and good inside, but Laura didn't. When she looked at Mary she wanted to slap her. So she dared not look at Mary again.

The beads made a beautiful string. Carrie clapped her hands and laughed

when she saw it. Then Ma tied it around Carrie's little neck, and it glittered there. Laura felt a little bit better. After all, her beads were not enough beads to make a whole string, and neither were Mary's, but together they made a whole string of beads for Carrie.

When Carrie felt the beads on her neck, she grabbed at them. She was so little that she did not know any better than to break the string. So Ma untied it, and she put the beads away until Carrie should be old enough to wear them. And often after that Laura thought of those pretty beads and she was still naughty enough to want her beads for herself.

But it had been a wonderful day. She could always think about that long walk across the prairie, and about all they had seen in the Indian camp.

The Wonders
of
Plum Creek

Soon it is time for the Ingalls family to move again. This time they settle in Minnesota and move into a dugout built into a grassy bank at the edge of Plum Creek. There are flowers growing all around their new home and a dirt path that leads down to the cold clear water. Every day when chores are done, Laura and Mary run outside to splash and play in the water and mud of the creek. Carrie is still a baby, so she must stay with Ma. These are special times for Laura and her sisters.

Straw-Stack

When Mr. Nelson's harvesting was done, Pa had paid for Spot. He could do his own harvesting now. He sharpened the long, dangerous scythe that little girls must never touch, and he cut down the wheat in the small field beyond the stable. He bound it in bundles and stacked them.

Then every morning he went to work on the level land across the creek. He cut the prairie grass and left it to dry in the sunshine. He raked it into piles with a wooden rake. He yoked Pete and Bright to the wagon, and he hauled the hay and made six big stacks of it over there.

At night he was always too tired, now, to play the fiddle. But he was glad because when the hay was stacked he could plow that stubble land, and that would be the wheat-field.

One morning at daylight three strange men came with a threshing-machine.

They threshed Pa's stack of wheat. Laura heard the harsh machinery noises while she drove Spot through the dewy grass, and when the sun rose chaff flew golden in the wind.

The threshing was done and the men went away with the machine before breakfast. Pa said he wished Hanson had sown more wheat.

"But there's enough to make us some flour," he said. "And the straw, with what hay I've cut, will feed the stock through the winter. Next year," he said, "we'll have a crop of wheat that will amount to something!"

When Laura and Mary went up on the prairie to play, that morning, the first thing they saw was a beautiful golden straw-stack.

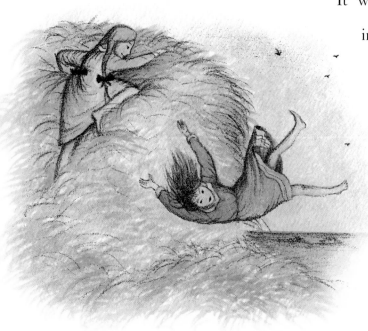

It was tall and shining bright in the sunshine. It smelled sweeter than hay.

Laura's feet slid in the sliding, slippery straw, but she could climb faster than straw slid. In a minute she was high on top of that stack.

She looked across the willow-tops and away beyond the creek at the far land. She could see the whole, great, round prairie. She was high up in the sky, almost as high as birds. Her arms waved and her feet bounced on the springy straw. She was almost flying, 'way high up in the windy sky.

"I'm flying! I'm flying!" she called down to Mary. Mary climbed up to her.

"Jump! Jump!" Laura said. They held hands and jumped, round and round, higher and higher. The wind blew and their skirts flapped and their sunbonnets swung at the ends of the sunbonnet strings around their necks.

"Higher! Higher!" Laura sang, jumping. Suddenly the straw slid under her. Over the edge of the stack she went, sitting in straw, sliding faster and faster. Bump! She landed at the bottom. Plump! Mary landed on her.

They rolled and laughed in the crackling straw. Then they climbed the stack, and slid down it again. They had never had so much fun.

They climbed up and slid, climbed and slid, until there was hardly any stack left in the middle of loose heaps of straw.

Then they were sober. Pa had made that straw-stack and now it was not at all as he had left it. Laura looked at Mary and Mary looked at her, and they looked at what was left of that straw-stack. Then Mary said she was going into the dugout, and Laura went quietly with her. They were very good, helping Ma and playing nicely with Carrie, until Pa came to dinner.

When he came in he looked straight at Laura, and Laura looked at the floor.

"You girls mustn't slide down the straw-stack any more," Pa said. "I had to stop and pitch up all that loose straw."

"We won't, Pa," Laura said, earnestly, and Mary said, "No, Pa, we won't."

After dinner Mary washed the dishes and Laura dried them. Then they put on their sunbonnets and went up the path to the prairie. The straw-stack was golden-bright in the sunshine.

"Laura! What are you doing!" said Mary.

"I'm not doing anything!" said Laura. "I'm not even hardly touching it!"

"You come right away from there, or I'll tell Ma!" said Mary.

"Pa didn't say I couldn't smell it," said Laura.

She stood close to the golden stack and sniffed long, deep sniffs. The straw was warmed by the sun. It smelled better than wheat kernels taste when you chew them. Laura burrowed her face in it, shutting her eyes and smelling deeper and deeper.

"Mmm!" she said.

Mary came and smelled it and said, "Mmm!"

Laura looked up the glistening, prickly, golden stack. She had never seen the sky so blue as it was above that gold. She could not stay on the ground. She had to be high up in that blue sky.

"Laura!" Mary cried. "Pa said we mustn't!"

Laura was climbing. "He did not, either!" she contradicted. "He did not say we must not climb up it. He said we must not slide down it. I'm only climbing."

"You come right straight down from there," said Mary.

Laura was on top of the stack. She looked down at Mary and said, like a very good little girl, "I am not going to slide down. Pa said not to."

Nothing but the blue sky was higher than she was. The wind was blowing. The green prairie was wide and far. Laura spread her arms and jumped, and the straw bounded her high.

"I'm flying! I'm flying!" she sang. Mary climbed up, and Mary began to fly, too.

They bounced until they could bounce no higher. Then they flopped flat on the sweet warm straw. Bulges of straw rose up on both sides of Laura. She rolled onto a bulge and it sank, but another rose up. She rolled onto that bulge, and then she was rolling faster and faster; she could not stop.

"Laura!" Mary screamed. "Pa said—" But Laura was rolling. Over, over, over, right down that straw-stack she rolled and thumped in straw on the ground.

She jumped up and climbed that straw-stack again as fast as she could. She flopped and began to roll again. "Come on, Mary!" she shouted. "Pa didn't say we can't roll!"

Mary stayed on top of the stack and argued. "I know Pa didn't say we can't roll, but—"

"Well, then!" Laura rolled down again. "Come on!" she called up. "It's lots of fun!"

"Well, but I—" said Mary. Then she came rolling down.

It was great fun. It was more fun than sliding. They climbed and rolled and climbed and rolled, laughing harder all the time. More and more straw rolled down with them. They waded in it and rolled each other in it and climbed and rolled down again, till there was hardly anything left to climb.

Then they brushed every bit of straw off their dresses, they picked every bit out of their hair, and they went quietly into the dugout.

When Pa came from the hay-field that night, Mary was busily setting the table for supper. Laura was behind the door, busy with the box of paper dolls.

"Laura," Pa said, dreadfully, "come here."

Slowly Laura went out from behind the door.

"Come here," said Pa, "right over here by Mary."

He sat down and he stood them before him, side by side. But it was Laura he looked at.

He said, sternly, "You girls have been sliding down the straw-stack again."

"No, Pa," said Laura.

"Mary!" said Pa. "Did you slide down the straw-stack?"

"N-no, Pa," Mary said.

"Laura!" Pa's voice was terrible. "Tell me again, DID YOU SLIDE DOWN THE STRAW-STACK?"

"No, Pa," Laura answered again. She looked straight into Pa's shocked eyes. She did not know why he looked like that.

"Laura!" Pa said.

"We did not slide, Pa," Laura explained. "But we did roll down it."

Pa got up quickly and went to the door and stood looking out. His back quivered. Laura and Mary did not know what to think.

When Pa turned around, his face was stern but his eyes were twinkling.

"All right, Laura," he said. "But now I want you girls to stay away from that straw-stack. Pete and Bright and Spot will have nothing but hay and straw to eat this winter. They need every bite of it. You don't want them to be hungry, do you?"

"Oh no, Pa!" they said.

"Well, if that straw's to be fit to feed them, it MUST—STAY—STACKED. Do you understand?"

"Yes, Pa," said Laura and Mary.

That was the end of their playing on the straw-stack.

Keeping House

Now in the daytimes Pa was driving the wagon up and down Plum Creek, and bringing load after load of logs to the pile by the door. He cut down old plum trees and old willows and cottonwoods, leaving the little ones to grow. He hauled them and stacked them, and chopped and split them into stove wood, till he had a big woodpile.

With his short-handled ax in his belt, his traps on his arm, and his gun against his shoulder, he walked far up Plum Creek, setting traps for muskrat and mink and otter and fox.

One evening at supper Pa said he had found a beaver meadow. But he did not

set traps there because so few beavers were left. He had seen a fox and shot at it, but missed.

"I am all out of practice hunting," he said. "It's a fine place we have here, but there isn't much game. Makes a fellow think of places out west where—"

"Where there are no schools for the children, Charles," said Ma.

"You're right, Caroline. You usually are," Pa said. "Listen to that wind. We'll have a storm tomorrow."

But the next day was mild as spring. The air was soft and warm and the sun shone brightly. In the middle of the morning Pa came to the house.

"Let's have an early dinner and take a walk to town this afternoon," he said to Ma. "This is too nice a day for you to stay indoors. Time enough for that when winter really comes."

"But the children," said Ma. "We can't take Carrie and walk so far."

"Shucks!" Pa laughed at her. "Mary and Laura are great girls now. They can take care of Carrie for one afternoon."

"Of course we can, Ma," said Mary; and Laura said, "Of course we can!"

They watched Pa and Ma starting gaily away. Ma was so pretty, in her brown-and-red Christmas shawl, with her brown knit hood tied under her chin, and she stepped so quickly and looked up at Pa so merrily that Laura thought she was like a bird.

Then Laura swept the floor while Mary cleared the table. Mary washed the dishes and Laura wiped them and put them in the cupboard. They put the red-checked cloth on the table. Now the whole long afternoon was before them and they could do as they pleased.

First, they decided to play school. Mary said she must be Teacher, because she was older and besides she knew more. Laura knew that was true. So Mary was Teacher and she liked it, but Laura was soon tired of that play.

"I know," Laura said. "Let's both teach Carrie her letters."

They sat Carrie on a bench and held the book before her, and both did their best. But Carrie did not like it. She would not learn the letters, so they had to stop that.

"Well," said Laura, "let's play keeping house."

"We *are* keeping house," said Mary. "What is the use of playing it?"

The house was empty and still, with Ma gone. Ma was so quiet and gentle that she never made any noise, but now the whole house was listening for her.

Laura went outdoors for a while by herself, but she came back. The afternoon grew longer and longer. There was nothing at all to do. Even Jack walked up and down restlessly.

He asked to go out, but when Laura opened the door he would not go. He lay

down and got up, and walked around and around the room. He came to Laura and looked at her earnestly.

"What is it, Jack!" Laura asked him. He stared hard at her, but she could not understand, and he almost howled.

"Don't, Jack!" Laura told him, quickly. "You scare me."

"Is it something outdoors?" Mary wondered. Laura ran out, but on the doorstep Jack took hold of her dress and pulled her back. Outdoors was bitter cold. Laura shut the door.

"Look," she said. "The sunshine's dark. Are the grasshoppers coming back?"

"Not in the winter-time, goosie," said Mary. "Maybe it's rain."

"Goosie yourself!" Laura said back. "It doesn't rain in the winter-time."

"Well, snow, then! What's the difference?" Mary was angry and so was Laura. They would have gone on quarreling, but suddenly there was no sunshine. They ran to look through the bedroom window.

A dark cloud with a fleecy white underside was rolling fast from the north-west.

Mary and Laura looked out the front window. Surely it was time for Pa and Ma to come, but they were nowhere in sight.

"Maybe it's a blizzard," said Mary.

"Like Pa told us about," said Laura.

They looked at each other through the gray air. They were thinking of those children who froze stark stiff.

"The woodbox is empty," said Laura.

Mary grabbed her. "You can't!" said Mary. "Ma told us to stay in the house if it stormed." Laura jerked away and Mary said, "Besides, Jack won't let you."

"We've got to bring in wood before the storm gets here," Laura told her. "Hurry!"

They could hear a strange sound in the wind, like a far-away screaming. They put on their shawls and pinned them under their chins with their large shawl-pins. They put on their mittens.

Laura was ready first. She told Jack, "We've got to bring in wood, Jack." He seemed to understand. He went out with her and stayed close at her heels. The wind was colder than icicles. Laura ran to the woodpile, piled up a big armful of wood, and ran back, with Jack behind her. She could not open the door while she held the wood. Mary opened it for her.

Then they did not know what to do. The cloud was coming swiftly, and they must both bring in wood before the storm got there. They could not open the door when their arms were full of wood. They could not leave the door open and let the cold come in.

"I tan open the door," said Carrie.

"You can't," Mary said.

"I tan, too!" said Carrie, and she reached up both hands and turned the door knob. She could do it! Carrie was big enough to open the door.

Laura and Mary hurried fast, bringing in wood. Carrie opened the door when they came to it, and shut it behind them. Mary could carry larger armfuls, but Laura was quicker.

They filled the woodbox before it began to snow. The snow came suddenly with a whirling blast, and it was small hard grains like sand. It stung Laura's face where it struck. When Carrie opened the door, it swirled into the house in a white cloud.

Laura and Mary forgot that Ma had told them to stay in the house when it stormed. They forgot everything but bringing in wood. They ran frantically back and forth, bringing each time all the wood they could stagger under.

They piled wood around the woodbox and around the stove. They piled it against the wall. They made the piles higher, and bigger.

Bang! they banged the door. They ran to the woodpile. Clop-clop-clop they stacked the wood on their arms. They ran to the door. Bump! it went open, and bang! they back-bumped it shut, and thumpity-thud-thump! they flung down the wood and ran back, outdoors, to the woodpile, and panting back again.

They could hardly see the woodpile in the swirling whiteness. Snow was

driven all in among the wood. They could hardly see the house, and Jack was a dark blob hurrying beside them. The hard snow scoured their faces. Laura's arms ached and her chest panted and all the time she thought, "Oh, where is Pa? Where is Ma?" and she felt "Hurry! Hurry!" and she heard the wind screeching.

The woodpile was gone. Mary took a few sticks and Laura took a few sticks

and there were no more. They ran to the door together, and Laura opened it and Jack bounded in. Carrie was at the front window, clapping her hands and squealing. Laura dropped her sticks of wood and turned just in time to see Pa and Ma burst, running, out of the whirling whiteness of snow.

Pa was holding Ma's hand and pulling to help her run. They burst into the house and slammed the door and stood panting, covered with snow. No one said anything while Pa and Ma looked at Laura and Mary, who stood all snowy in shawls and mittens.

At last Mary said in a small voice, "We did go out in the storm, Ma. We forgot."

Laura's head bowed down and she said, "We didn't want to burn up the furniture, Pa, and freeze stark stiff."

"Well, I'll be darned!" said Pa. "If they didn't move the whole woodpile in. All the wood I cut to last a couple of weeks."

There, piled up in the house, was the whole woodpile. Melted snow was leaking out of it and spreading in puddles. A wet path went to the door, where snow lay unmelted.

Then Pa's great laugh rang out, and Ma's gentle smile shone warm on Mary and Laura. They knew they were forgiven for disobeying, because they had been wise to bring in wood, though perhaps not quite so much wood.

Sometime soon they would be old enough not to make any mistakes, and then they could always decide what to do. They would not have to obey Pa and Ma any more.

They bustled to take off Ma's shawl and hood and brush the snow from them and hang them up to dry. Pa hurried to the stable to do the chores before the storm grew worse. Then while Ma rested, they stacked the wood neatly as she told them, and they swept and mopped the floor.

The house was neat and cosy again. The tea-kettle hummed, the fire shone brightly from the draughts above the stove hearth. Snow swished against the windows.

Pa came in. "Here is the little milk I could get here with. The wind blew it up out of the pail. Caroline, this is a terrible storm. I couldn't see an inch, and the wind comes from all directions at once. I thought I was on the path, but I couldn't see the house, and—well, I just barely bumped against the corner. Another foot to the left and I never would have got in."

"*Charles!*" Ma said.

"Nothing to be scared about now," said Pa. "But if we hadn't run all the way from town and beat this storm here—" Then his eyes twinkled, he rumpled Mary's hair and pulled Laura's ear. "I'm glad all this wood is in the house, too," he said.

Silver Lake Adventure

After Plum Creek the Ingallses move west again in hopes of finding unsettled wilderness. They decide to start a new life in De Smet, South Dakota. By now Laura and Mary are becoming young ladies, and Carrie is no longer the baby of the family. Baby Grace is the new little sister in the Ingalls family. Times are busy for Laura. Scarlet fever has left Mary blind, but Laura is always there for her sister, ready to be her eyes and describe all the beauty that surrounds them. And there is always mischievous baby Grace for Laura to look after. Life at Silver Lake isn't always easy for Laura and her sisters, but it is always full of surprises!

Where Violets Grow

Laura was running straight toward the south. Grass whipped soft against her bare feet. Butterflies fluttered over the flowers. There wasn't a bush nor a weed that Grace could be hidden behind. There was nothing, nothing but grass and flowers swaying in the sunshine.

If she were little and playing all by herself, Laura thought, she wouldn't go into the dark Big Slough, she wouldn't go into the mud and the tall grass. "Oh, Grace, why didn't I watch you?" she thought. Sweet pretty little helpless sister— "Grace! Grace!" she screamed. Her breath caught and hurt in her side.

She ran on and on. "Grace must have gone this way. Maybe she chased a butterfly. She didn't go into Big Slough! She didn't climb the hill, she wasn't there. Oh, baby sister, I couldn't see you anywhere east or south on this hateful prairie." "Grace!"

The horrible, sunny prairie was so large. No lost baby could ever be found on it. Ma's calling and Pa's shouts came from Big Slough. They were thin cries, lost in wind, lost on the enormous bigness of the prairie.

Laura's breathing hurt her sides under the ribs. Her chest was smothering and her eyes were dizzy. She ran up a low slope. Nothing, nothing, not a spot of shadow was anywhere on the level prairie all around her. She ran on, and suddenly the ground dropped before her. She almost fell down a steep bank.

There was Grace. There, in a great pool of blue, sat Grace. The sun shone on her golden hair blowing in the wind. She looked up at Laura with big eyes as blue as violets. Her hands were full of violets. She held them up to Laura and said, "Sweet! Sweet!"

Laura sank down and took Grace in her arms. She held Grace carefully and panted for breath. Grace leaned over her arm to reach more violets. They were surrounded by masses of violets blossoming above low-spreading leaves. Violets covered the flat bottom of a large, round hollow. All around this lake of violets, grassy banks rose almost straight up to the prairie-level. There in the round, low place the wind hardly disturbed the fragrance of the violets. The sun was warm there, the sky was overhead, the green walls of grass curved all around, and butterflies fluttered over the crowding violet-faces.

Laura stood up and lifted Grace to her feet. She took the violets that Grace

gave her, and clasped her hand. "Come, Grace," she said. "We must go home."

She gave one look around the little hollow while she helped Grace climb the bank.

Grace walked so slowly that for a little while Laura carried her. Then she let her walk, for Grace was nearly three years old, and heavy. Then she lifted her again. So, carrying Grace and helping her walk, Laura brought her to the shanty and gave her to Mary.

Then she ran toward the Big Slough, calling as she ran. "Pa! Ma! She's here!" She kept on calling until Pa heard her and shouted to Ma, far in the tall grass. Slowly, together, they fought their way out of Big Slough and slowly came up to the shanty, draggled and muddy and very tired and thankful.

"Where did you find her, Laura?" Ma asked, taking Grace in her arms and sinking into her chair.

"In a—" Laura hesitated, and said, "Pa, could it really be a fairy ring? It is perfectly round. The bottom is perfectly flat. The bank around it is the same height all the way. You can't see a sign of that place till you stand on the bank. It is very large, and the whole bottom of it is covered solidly thick with violets. A place like that couldn't just happen, Pa. Something made it."

"You are too old to be believing in fairies, Laura," Ma said gently. "Charles, you must not encourage such fancies."

"But it isn't—it isn't like a real place, truly," Laura protested. "And smell how sweet the violets are. They aren't like ordinary violets."

"They do make the whole house sweet," Ma admitted. "But they are real violets, and there are no fairies."

"You are right, Laura; human hands didn't make that place," Pa said. "But your fairies were big, ugly brutes, with horns on their heads and humps on their backs. That place is an old buffalo wallow. You know buffaloes are wild cattle. They paw up the ground and wallow in the dust, just as cattle do.

"For ages the buffalo herds had these wallowing places. They pawed up the ground and the wind blew the dust away. Then another herd came along and pawed up more dust in the same place. They went always to the same places, and—"

"Why did they, Pa?" Laura asked.

"I don't know," Pa said. "Maybe because the ground was mellowed there. Now the buffalo are gone, and grass grows over their wallows. Grass and violets."

"Well," Ma said. "All's well that ends well, and here it is long past dinnertime. I hope you and Carrie didn't let the biscuits burn, Mary."

"No, Ma," Mary said, and Carrie showed her the biscuits wrapped in a clean cloth to keep warm, and the potatoes drained and mealy-dry in their pot. And Laura said, "Sit still, Ma, and rest. I'll fry the salt pork and make the gravy."

No one but Grace was hungry. They ate slowly, and then Pa finished planting the windbreak. Ma helped Grace hold her own little tree while Pa set it firmly. When all the trees were planted, Carrie and Laura gave them each a full pail of water from the well. Before they finished, it was time to help get supper.

"Well," Pa said at the table. "We're settled at last on our homestead claim."

"Yes," said Ma. "All but one thing. Mercy, what a day this has been. I didn't get time to drive the nail for the bracket."

"I'll tend to it, Caroline, as soon as I drink my tea," Pa said.

He took the hammer from his toolbox under the bed, and drove a nail into the wall between the table and the whatnot. "Now bring on your bracket and the china shepherdess!" he said.

Ma brought them to him. He hung the bracket on the nail and stood the china shepherdess on its shelf. Her little china shoes, her tight china bodice and her golden hair were as bright as they had been so long ago in the Big Woods. Her china skirts were as wide and white; her cheeks as pink and her blue eyes as sweet as ever. And the bracket that Pa had carved for Ma's Christmas present so long ago was still without a scratch, and even more glossily polished than when it was new.

Over the door Pa hung his rifle and his shotgun, and then he hung on a nail above them a bright, new horseshoe.

"Well," he said, looking around at the snugly crowded shanty. "A short horse is soon curried. This is our tightest squeeze yet, Caroline, but it's only a beginning." Ma's eyes smiled into his eyes, and he said to Laura, "I could sing you a song about that horseshoe."

She brought him the fiddle box, and he sat down in the doorway and tuned the fiddle. Ma settled in her chair to rock Grace to sleep. Softly Laura washed the dishes and Carrie wiped them while Pa played the fiddle and sang.

> *"We journey along quite contented in life*
>
> *And try to live peaceful with all.*
>
> *We keep ourselves free from all trouble and strife*
>
> *And we're glad when our friends on us call.*
>
> *Our home it is happy and cheerful and bright,*
>
> *We're content and we ask nothing more.*
>
> *And the reason we prosper, I'll tell to you now,*
>
> *There's a horseshoe hung over the door:*
>
> *"Keep the horseshoe hung over the door!*
>
> *It will bring you good luck evermore.*
>
> *If you would be happy and free from all care,*
>
> *Keep the horseshoe hung over the door!"*

"It sounds rather heathenish to me, Charles," Ma said.

"Well, anyway," Pa replied, "I wouldn't wonder if we do pretty well here, Caroline. In time we'll build more rooms on this house, and maybe have a driving team and buggy. I'm not going to plow up much grass. We'll have a garden and a little field, but mostly raise hay and cattle. Where so many buffalo ranged, must be a good country for cattle."

The dishes were done. Laura carried the dishpan some distance from the back door and flung the water far over the grass where tomorrow's sun would dry it. The first stars were pricking through the pale sky. A few lights twinkled yellow in the little town, but the whole great plain of the earth was shadowy. There was hardly a wind, but the air moved and whispered to itself in the grasses. Laura almost knew what it said. Lonely and wild and eternal were land and water and sky and the air blowing.

"The buffalo are gone," Laura thought. "And now we're homesteaders."

Sisters
in the
Little Town

After a cold and dangerous October blizzard, the Ingallses move to town for the winter. But when springtime comes, it's back to their homestead claim and the sweet Dakota prairie land Laura and her sisters love. By now Laura is almost fifteen, Mary is sixteen, Carrie is ten, and Grace is a toddler. When Laura isn't helping Pa build their new home on the prairie, she and Mary take long walks and talk about the special times they shared growing up together. Carrie's days are spent minding curious little Grace, who is delighted by the wonders of the open prairie that unfold before her eyes.

Springtime on the Claim

After the October Blizzard last fall, they had all moved to town and for a little while Laura had gone to school there. Then the storms had stopped school, and all through that long winter the blizzards had howled between the houses, shutting them off from each other so that day after day and night after night not a voice could be heard and not a light could be seen through the whirling snow.

All winter long, they had been crowded in the little kitchen, cold and hungry and working hard in the dark and the cold to twist enough hay to keep the fire going and to grind wheat in the coffee mill for the day's bread.

All that long, long winter, the only hope had been that sometime winter must end, sometime blizzards must stop, the sun would shine warm again and they

could all get away from the town and go back to the homestead claim.

Now it was springtime. The Dakota prairie lay so warm and bright under the shining sun that it did not seem possible that it had ever been swept by the winds and snows of that hard winter. How wonderful it was, to be on the claim again! Laura wanted nothing more than just being outdoors. She felt she never could get enough sunshine soaked into her bones.

In the dawns when she went to the well at the edge of the slough to fetch the morning pail of fresh water, the sun was rising in a glory of colors. Meadow larks were flying, singing, up from the dew-wet grass. Jack rabbits hopped beside the path, their bright eyes watching and their long ears twitching as they daintily nibbled their breakfast of tender grass tips.

Laura was in the shanty only long enough to set down the water and snatch the milk pail. She ran out to the slope where Ellen, the cow, was cropping the sweet young grass. Quietly Ellen stood chewing her cud while Laura milked.

Warm and sweet, the scent of new milk came up from the streams hissing into the rising foam, and it mixed with the scents of springtime. Laura's bare feet were wet and cool in the dewy grass, the sunshine was warm on her neck, and Ellen's flank was warmer against her cheek. On its own little picket rope, Ellen's baby calf bawled anxiously, and Ellen answered with a soothing moo.

When Laura had stripped the last creamy drops of milk, she lugged the pail to the shanty. Ma poured some of the warm new milk into the calf's pail. The rest she strained through a clean white cloth into tin milk pans, and Laura carefully carried them down cellar while Ma skimmed thick cream from last night's milk. Then she poured the skimmed milk into the calf's pail, and Laura carried it to the hungry calf.

Teaching the calf to drink was not easy, but always interesting. The wobbly-legged baby calf had been born believing that it must butt hard with its little red poll, to get milk. So when it smelled the milk in the pail, it tried to butt the pail.

Laura must keep it from spilling the milk, if she could, and she had to teach it how to drink, because it didn't know. She dipped her fingers into the milk and let the calf's rough tongue suck them, and gently she led its nose down to the milk in the pail. The calf suddenly snorted milk into its nose, sneezed it out with a whoosh that splashed milk out of the pail, and then with all its might it butted into the milk. It butted so hard that Laura almost lost hold of the pail. A wave of milk went over the calf's head and a splash wet the front of Laura's dress.

So, patiently she began again, dipping her fingers for the calf to suck, trying to keep the milk in the pail and to teach the calf to drink it. In the end, some of the milk was inside the calf.

Then Laura pulled up the picket pins. One by one, she led Ellen, the baby calf and the yearling calf to fresh places in the soft, cool grass. She drove the iron pins deep into the ground. The sun was fully up now, the whole sky was blue, and the whole earth was waves of grass flowing in the wind. And Ma was calling.

"Hurry, Laura! Breakfast's waiting!"

In the shanty, Laura quickly washed her face and hands at the washbasin. She threw out the water in a sparkling curve falling on grass where the sun would

swiftly dry it. She ran the comb through her hair, over her head to the dangling braid. There was never time before breakfast to undo the long braid, brush her hair properly, and plait it again. She would do that after the morning's work was done.

Sitting in her place beside Mary, she looked across the clean, red-checked tablecloth and the glinting dishes at little sister Carrie and baby sister Grace, with their soap-shining morning faces and bright eyes. She looked at Pa and Ma so cheerful and smiling. She felt the sweet morning wind from the wide-open door and window, and she gave a little sigh.

Pa looked at her. He knew how she felt. "I think, myself, it's pretty nice," he said.

"It's a beautiful morning," Ma agreed.

Then after breakfast Pa hitched up the horses, Sam and David, and drove them out on the prairie east of the shanty, where he was breaking ground for sod corn. Ma took charge of the day's work for the rest of them, and best of all Laura liked the days when she said, "I must work in the garden."

Mary eagerly offered to do all the housework, so that Laura could help Ma. Mary was blind. Even in the days before scarlet fever had taken the sight from her clear blue eyes, she had never liked to work outdoors in the sun and wind. Now she was happy to be useful indoors. Cheerfully she said, "I must work where I can see with my fingers. I couldn't tell the difference between a pea

vine and a weed at the end of a hoe, but I can wash dishes and make beds and take care of Grace."

Carrie was proud, too, because although she was small she was ten years old and could help Mary do all the housework. So Ma and Laura went out to work in the garden.

People were coming from the East now, to settle all over the prairie. They were building new claim shanties to the east and to the south, and west beyond Big Slough. Every few days a wagon went by, driven by strangers going across the neck of the slough and northward to town, and coming back. Ma said there would be time to get acquainted when the spring work was done. There is no time for visiting in the spring.

Pa had a new plow, a breaking plow. It was wonderful for breaking the prairie sod. It had a sharp-edged wheel, called a rolling coulter, that ran rolling and cutting through the sod ahead of the plowshare. The sharp steel plowshare followed it, slicing underneath the matted grass roots, and the moldboard lifted the long, straight-edged strip of sod and turned it upside down. The strip of sod was exactly twelve inches wide, and as straight as if it had been cut by hand.

They were all so happy about that new plow. Now, after a whole day's work, Sam and David gaily lay down and rolled, and pricked their ears and looked about the prairie before they fell to cropping grass. They were not being worn down,

sad and gaunt, by breaking sod that spring. And at supper, Pa was not too tired to joke.

"By jingo, that plow can handle the work by itself," he said. "With all these new inventions nowadays, there's no use for a man's muscle. One of these nights that plow'll take a notion to keep on going, and we'll look out in the morning and see that it's turned over an acre or two after the team and I quit for the night."

The strips of sod lay bottom-side-up over the furrows, with all the cut-off grass roots showing speckled in the earth. The fresh furrow was delightfully cool and soft to bare feet, and often Carrie and Grace followed behind the plow, playing. Laura would have liked to, but she was going on fifteen years old now, too old to play in the fresh, clean-smelling dirt. Besides, in the afternoons Mary must go for a walk to get some sunshine.

So when the morning's work was done, Laura took Mary walking over the prairie. Spring flowers were blossoming and cloud-shadows were trailing over the grassy slopes.

It was odd that when they were little, Mary had been the older and often bossy, but now that they were older they seemed to be the same age. They liked the long walks together in the wind and sunshine, picking violets and buttercups and eating sheep sorrel. The sheep sorrel's lovely curled lavender blossoms, the clover-shaped leaves and thin stems had a tangy taste.

"Sheep sorrel tastes like springtime," Laura said.

"It really tastes a little like lemon flavoring, Laura," Mary gently corrected her. Before she ate sheep sorrel she always asked, "Did you look carefully? You're sure there isn't a bug on it?"

"There never are any bugs," Laura protested. "These prairies are so *clean!* There never was such a clean place."

"You look, just the same," said Mary. "I don't want to eat the only bug in the whole of Dakota Territory."

They laughed together. Mary was so light-hearted now that she often made such little jokes. Her face was so serene in her sunbonnet, her blue eyes were so clear and her voice so gay that she did not seem to be walking in darkness.

Mary had always been good. Sometimes she had been so good that Laura could hardly bear it. But now she seemed different. Once Laura asked her about it.

"You used to try all the time to be good," Laura said. "And you always were good. It made me so mad sometimes, I wanted to slap you. But now you are good without even trying."

Mary stopped still. "Oh, Laura, how awful! Do you ever want to slap me now?"

"No, never," Laura answered honestly.

"You honestly don't? You aren't just being gentle to me because I'm blind?"

"No! Really and honestly, no, Mary. I hardly think about your being blind. I—I'm just glad you're my sister. I wish I could be like you. But I guess I never can be," Laura sighed. "I don't know how you can be so good."

"I'm not really," Mary told her. "I do try, but if you could see how rebellious and mean I feel sometimes, if you could see what I really am, inside, you wouldn't want to be like me."

"I *can* see what you're like inside," Laura contradicted. "It shows all the time. You're always perfectly patient and never the least bit mean."

"I know why you wanted to slap me," Mary said. "It was because I was showing off. I wasn't really wanting to be good. I was showing off to myself, what a good little girl I was, and being vain and proud, and I deserved to be slapped for it."

Laura was shocked. Then suddenly she felt that she had known that, all the time. But, nevertheless, it was not true of Mary. She said, "Oh no, you're not like that, not really. You *are* good."

"We are all desperately wicked and inclined to evil as the sparks fly upwards," said Mary, using the Bible words. "But that doesn't matter."

"What!" cried Laura.

"I mean I don't believe we ought to think so much about ourselves, about whether we are bad or good," Mary explained.

"But, my goodness! How can anybody be good without thinking about it?" Laura demanded.

"I don't know, I guess we couldn't," Mary admitted. "I don't know how to say what I mean very well. But—it isn't so much thinking, as—as just knowing. Just being sure of the goodness of God."

Laura stood still, and so did Mary, because she dared not step without Laura's arm in hers guiding her. There Mary stood in the midst of the green and flowery miles of grass rippling in the wind, under the great blue sky and white clouds sailing, and she could not see. Everyone knows that God is good. But it seemed to Laura then that Mary must be sure of it in some special way.

"You are sure, aren't you?" Laura said.

"Yes, I am sure of it now all the time," Mary answered. "The Lord is my shepherd, I shall not want. He maketh me to lie down in green pastures, He leadeth me beside the still waters. I think that's the loveliest Psalm of all. Why are we stopping here? I don't smell the violets."

"We came by the buffalo wallow, talking," said Laura. "We'll go back that way."

When they turned back, Laura could see the low swell of land sloping up from the coarse grasses of Big Slough to the little claim shanty. It looked hardly larger than a hen coop, with its half-roof slanting up and stopping. The sod stable hardly showed in the wild grasses. Beyond them Ellen and the two calves were grazing, and to the east Pa was planting corn in the newly broken sod.

He had broken all the sod he had time to, before the ground grew too dry. He had harrowed the ground he had broken last year, and sowed it to oats. Now with a sack of seed corn fastened to a shoulder harness, and the hoe in his hand, he was going slowly across the sod field.

"Pa is planting the corn," Laura told Mary. "Let's go by that way. Here's the buffalo wallow now."

"I know," said Mary. They stood a moment, breathing in deeply the perfume of warm violets that came up as thick as honey. The buffalo wallow, perfectly round and set down into the prairie like a dish three or four feet deep, was solidly paved with violets. Thousands, millions, crowded so thickly that they hid their own leaves.

Mary sank down among them. "Mmmmmm!" she breathed. Her fingers delicately felt over the masses of petals, and down the thin stems to pick them.

When they passed by the sod field Pa breathed in a deep smell of the violets, too. "Had a nice walk, girls?" he smiled at them, but he did not stop working. He mellowed a spot of earth with the hoe, dug a tiny hollow in it, dropped four kernels of corn in the hollow, covered them with the hoe,

pressed the spot firm with his boot, then stepped on to plant the next hill.

Carrie came hurrying to bury her nose in the violets.

She was minding Grace, and Grace would play nowhere but in the field where Pa was. Angleworms fascinated Grace. Every time Pa struck the hoe into the ground she watched for one, and chuckled to see the thin, long worm make itself fat and short, pushing itself quickly into the earth again.

"Even when it's cut in two, both halves do that," she said. "Why, Pa?"

"They want to get into the ground, I guess," said Pa.

"Why, Pa?" Grace asked him.

"Oh, they just want to," said Pa.

"Why do they want to, Pa?"

"Why do you like to play in the dirt?" Pa asked her.

"Why, Pa?" Grace said. "How many corns do you drop, Pa?"

"Kernels," said Pa. "Four kernels. One, two, three, four."

"One, two, four," Grace said. "Why, Pa?"

"That's an easy one," said Pa.

> *"One for the blackbird,*
>
> *One for the crow,*
>
> *And that will leave*
>
> *Just two to grow."*

The garden was growing now. In tiny rows of different greens, the radishes, lettuce, onions, were up. The first crumpled leaves of peas were pushing upward. The young tomatoes stood on thin stems, spreading out their first lacy foliage.

"I've been looking at the garden, it needs hoeing," Ma said, while Laura set the violets in water to perfume the supper table. "And I do believe the beans will be up any day now, it's turned so warm."

All one hot morning, the beans were popping out of the ground. Grace discovered them and came shrieking with excitement to tell Ma. All that morning she could not be coaxed away from watching them. Up from the bare earth, bean after bean was popping, its stem uncoiling like a steel spring, and up in the sunshine the halves of the split bean still clutched two pale twin-leaves. Every time a bean popped up, Grace squealed again.

Now that the corn was planted, Pa built the missing half of the claim shanty. One morning he laid the floor joists. Then he made the frame, and Laura helped him raise it and hold it straight to the plumb line while he nailed it. He put in the studding, and the frames for two windows. Then he laid the rafters, to make the other slant of the roof that had not been there before.

Laura helped him all the time, Carrie and Grace watched, and picked up every nail that Pa dropped by mistake. Even Ma often spent minutes in idleness, looking on. It was exciting to see the shanty being made into a house.

When it was done, they had three rooms. The new part was two tiny bedrooms, each with a window. Now the beds would not be in the front room any more.

"Here's where we kill two birds with one stone," said Ma. "We'll combine spring housecleaning and moving."

They washed the window curtains and all the quilts and hung them out to dry. Then they washed the new windows till they shone, and hung on them new curtains made of old sheets and beautifully hemmed with Mary's tiny stitches. Ma and Laura set up the bedsteads in the new rooms all made of fresh, clean-smelling boards. Laura and Carrie filled the straw ticks with the brightest hay from the middle of a haystack, and they made up the beds with sheets still warm from Ma's ironing and with the clean quilts smelling of the prairie air.

Then Ma and Laura scrubbed and scoured every inch of the old shanty, that was now the front room. It was spacious now, with no beds in it, only the cookstove and cupboards and table and chairs and the whatnot. When it was perfectly clean, and everything in place, they all stood and admired it.

"You needn't see it for me, Laura," Mary said. "I can feel how large and fresh and pretty it is."

The fresh, starched white curtains moved softly in the wind at the open window. The scrubbed board walls and the floor were a soft yellow-gray. A

bouquet of grass flowers and windflowers that Carrie had picked and put in the blue bowl on the table, seemed to bring springtime in. In the corner the varnished brown whatnot stood stylish and handsome.

The afternoon light made plain the gilded titles of the books on the whatnot's lower shelf, and glittered in the three glass boxes on the shelf above, each with tiny flowers painted on it. Above them, on the next shelf, the gilt flowers shone on the glass face of the clock and its brass pendulum glinted, swinging to and fro. Higher still, on the very top shelf, was Laura's white china jewel box with the wee gold cup and saucer on its lid, and beside it, watching over it, sat Carrie's brown and white china dog.

On the wall between the doors of the new bedrooms, Ma hung the wooden bracket that Pa had carved for her Christmas present, long ago in the Big Woods of Wisconsin. Every little flower and leaf, the small vine on the edge of the little shelf, and the larger vines climbing to the large star at the top, were still as perfect as when he had carved them with his jackknife. Older still, older than Laura could remember, Ma's china shepherdess stood pink and white and smiling on the shelf.

It was a beautiful room.

Remembering the Golden Years

Laura is almost sixteen now and working hard teaching school. It isn't easy for her, but she's ready to do her best to earn enough money to let Mary attend a college for the blind. Laura is living away from home while teaching, and Mary is away at school studying. For the first time ever, the Ingalls sisters are separated. But the day has finally come when both Laura and Mary will be home with Ma and Pa and their sisters, Carrie and Grace. The Ingalls sisters are reunited once again!

Mary Comes Home

Laura was so glad to be at home again, out on Pa's claim. It was good to milk the cow, and to drink all she wanted of milk, and to spread butter on her bread, and eat again of Ma's good cottage cheese. There were lettuce leaves to be picked in the garden, too, and little red radishes. She had not realized that she was so hungry for these good things to eat. Mrs. McKee and Mattie could not get them, of course, while they were holding down their claim.

At home now there were eggs, too, for Ma's flock was doing well. Laura helped Carrie hunt for nests that the hens hid in the hay at the stable and in the tall grass nearby.

Grace found a nest of kittens hidden in the manger. They were grandchildren of the little kitten that Pa had bought for fifty cents, and Kitty felt her responsibility.

She thought that she should hunt for them as well as for her own kittens. She brought in more gophers than all of them could eat, and every day she piled the extra ones by the house door for Ma.

"I declare," Ma said, "I never was so embarrassed by a cat's generosity."

The day came when Mary was coming home. Pa and Ma drove to town to fetch her, and even the train seemed special that afternoon as it came at last, unrolling its black smoke into a melting line low on the sky. From the rise of ground behind the stable and the garden, they saw the white steam puff up from its engine and heard its whistle; its far rumbling was still, and they knew that it had stopped in town and that Mary must be there now.

What excitement there was when at last the wagon came up from the slough, with Mary sitting on the seat between Pa and Ma. Laura and Carrie both talked at once and Mary tried to talk to both at the same time. Grace was in everyone's way, her hair flying and her blue eyes wide. Kitty went out through the doorway like a streak, with her tail swelled to a big brush. Kitty did not like strangers, and she had forgotten Mary.

"Weren't you afraid to come all by yourself on the cars?" Carrie asked.

"Oh, no," Mary smiled. "I had no trouble. We like to do things by ourselves, at college. It is part of our education."

She did seem much more sure of herself, and she moved easily around the

house, instead of sitting quiet in her chair. Pa brought in her trunk, and she went to it, knelt down and unlocked and opened it quite as if she saw it. Then she took from it, one after another, the presents she had brought.

For Ma there was a lamp mat of woven braid, with a fringe all around it of many-colored beads strung on stout thread.

"It is beautiful," Ma said in delight.

Laura's gift was a bracelet of blue and white beads strung on thread and woven together, and Carrie's was a ring of pink and white beads interwoven.

"Oh, how pretty! how pretty!" Carrie exclaimed. "And it fits, too; it fits perfectly!"

For Grace there was a little doll's chair, of red and green beads strung on wire. Grace was so overcome as she took it carefully into her hands that she could hardly say thank you to Mary.

"This is for you, Pa," Mary said, as she gave him a blue silk handkerchief. "I didn't make this, but I chose it myself. Blanche and I . . . Blanche is my roommate. We went downtown to find something for you. She can see colors if they are bright, but the clerk didn't know it. We thought it would be fun to mystify him, so Blanche signaled the colors to me, and he thought we could tell them by touch. I knew by the feeling that it was good silk. My, we did fool that clerk!" and, remembering, Mary laughed.

Mary had often smiled, but it was a long time since they had heard her laugh out, as she used to when she was a little girl. All that it had cost to send Mary to college was more than repaid by seeing her so gay and confident.

"I'll bet this was the prettiest handkerchief in Vinton, Iowa!" Pa said.

"I don't see how you put the right colors into your beadwork," Laura said, turning the bracelet on her wrist. "Every little bead in this lovely bracelet is right. You can't do that by fooling a clerk."

"Some seeing person puts the different colors in separate boxes," Mary explained. "Then we only have to remember where they are."

"You can do that easily," Laura agreed. "You always could remember things. You know I never could say as many Bible verses as you."

"It surprises my Sunday School teacher now, how many of them I know," said Mary. "Knowing them was a great help to me, Ma. I could read them so easily with my fingers in raised print and in Braille, that I learned how to read everything sooner than anyone else in my class."

"I am glad to know that, Mary," was all that Ma said, and her smile trembled, but she looked happier than when Mary had given her the beautiful lamp mat.

"Here is my Braille slate," said Mary, lifting it from her trunk. It was an oblong of thin steel in a steel frame, as large as a school slate, with a narrow steel band across it. The band was cut into several rows of open squares, and it would slide up and down,

or could be fastened in place at any point. Tied to the frame by a string was a pencil-shaped piece of steel that Mary said was a stylus.

"How do you use it?" Pa wanted to know.

"Watch and I'll show you," said Mary.

They all watched while she laid a sheet of thick, cream-colored paper on the slate, under the slide. She moved the slide to the top of the frame and secured it there. Then with the point of the stylus she pressed, rapidly, here and there in the corners of the open squares.

"There," she said, slipping the paper out and turning it over. Wherever the stylus had pressed, there was a tiny bump, that could easily be felt with the fingers. The bumps made different patterns, the size of the squares, and these were the Braille letters.

"I am writing to Blanche to tell her that I am safely home," said Mary. "I must write to my teacher, too." She turned the paper over, put it in the frame again, and slipped the slide down, ready to go on writing on the blank space. "I will finish them later."

"It is wonderful that you can write to your friends and they can read your letters," said Ma. "I can hardly believe that you are really getting the college education that we always wanted you to have."

Laura was so happy that she felt like crying, too.

"Well, well," Pa broke in. "Here we stand talking, when Mary must be hungry and it's chore time. Let's do our work now, and we will have longer to talk afterward."

"You are right, Charles," Ma quickly agreed. "Supper will be ready by the time you are ready for it."

While Pa took care of the horses, Laura hurried to do the milking and Carrie made a quick fire to bake the biscuit that Ma was mixing.

Supper was ready when Pa came from the stable and Laura had strained the milk.

It was a happy family, all together again, as they ate of the browned hashed potatoes, poached fresh eggs and delicious biscuit with Ma's good butter. Pa and Ma drank their fragrant tea, but Mary drank milk with the other girls. "It is a treat," she said. "We don't have such good milk at college."

There was so much to ask and tell that almost nothing was fully said, but tomorrow would be another long day with Mary. And it was like old times again, when Laura and Mary went to sleep as they used to, in their bed where Laura for so long had been sleeping alone.

"It's warm weather," Mary said, "so I won't be putting my cold feet on you as I used to do."

"I'm so glad you're here that I wouldn't complain," Laura answered. "It would be a pleasure."